We Are Cousins
Somos Primos

By / Por Diane Gonzales Bertrand
Illustrated by / Ilustraciones de Christina E. Rodriguez

Piñata Books
Arte Público Press
Houston, Texas

Publication of *We Are Cousins* is funded in part by grants from the city of Houston through the Houston Arts Alliance, the Clayton Fund, and the Exemplar Program, a program of Americans for the Arts in collaboration with the LarsonAllen Public Services Group, funded by the Ford Foundation. We are grateful for their support.

La publicación de *Somos primos* ha sido subvencionada en parte por la ciudad de Houston a través del Houston Arts Alliance, el Fondo Clayton y el Exemplar Program, un programa de Americans for the Arts en colaboración con el LarsonAllen Public Services Group, fundado por la Fundación Ford. Agradecemos su apoyo.

Piñata Books are full of surprises!
¡Piñata Books están llenos de sorpresas!

Piñata Books
An Imprint of Arte Público Press
University of Houston
452 Cullen Performance Hall
Houston, Texas 77204-2004

Bertrand, Diane Gonzales.
  We are cousins = Somos primos / by Diane Gonzales Bertrand ; with illustrations by Christina Rodriguez.
    p. cm.
  ISBN-13: 978-1-55885-502-1 (alk. paper) (paperback)
  ISBN-13: 978-1-55885-486-4 (alk. paper) (hardcover)
  I. Rodriguez, Christina. II. Title. III. Title: Somos primos.
  PZ73.B449 2007
  [E]—dc22
                                                                                2007061476

♾ The paper used in this publication meets the requirements of the American National Standard for Permanence of Paper for Printed Library Materials Z39.48-1984.

7 8 9 0 1 2 3 4 5 6   0 9 8 7 6 5 4 3 2 1

We are cousins.

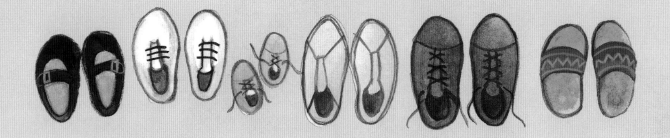

Somos primos.

Our mothers are sisters.

Nuestras madres son hermanas.

We have to share Grandpa's lap.

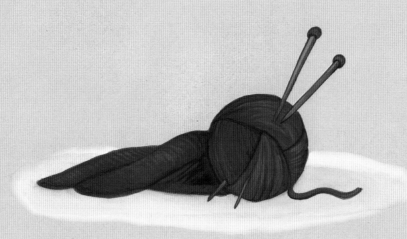

Tenemos que compartir el regazo de Abuelo.

We look like each other.

Nos parecemos.

We pass around clothes that don't fit anymore.

Nos intercambiamos la ropa que ya no nos queda.

We celebrate our birthdays together.

Celebramos nuestros cumpleaños juntos.

We sing and dance in make-believe parades.

Cantamos y bailamos en nuestros desfiles de mentira.

We blame each other when something goes wrong.

Nos culpamos cuando pasa algo malo.

We enjoy sharing a big pizza.

Nos gusta compartir una pizza grande.

But we don't always share our toys.

Pero no siempre compartimos nuestros juguetes.

We sleep over at each other's homes.

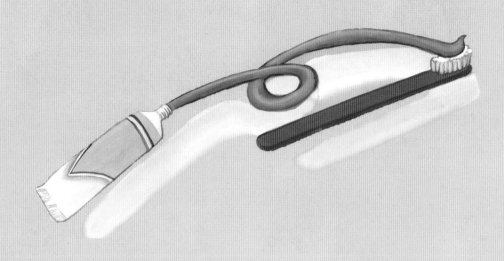

Dormimos en las casas de unos y otros.

We all fit inside one of Grandma's hugs.

Todos cabemos dentro de uno de los abrazos de Abuela.

We are cousins.

Somos primos.

We are family.

Somos familia.

Diane Gonzales Bertrand comes from a big family of cousins who played together as children. She watched her nieces and nephews enjoy the same relationship and decided to celebrate family togetherness with this story. Bertrand also wrote *Family, Familia,* a book about two cousins who meet at a family reunion, and two delicious books about food and family: *Sip, Slurp, Soup, Soup / Caldo, caldo, caldo* and *The Empanadas that Abuela Made / Las Empanadas que hacía la abuela.* She lives in San Antonio, Texas with her wonderful family.

Diane Gonzales Bertrand viene de una familia de muchos primos que jugaban juntos cuando eran niños. Vio que sus sobrinas y sobrinos disfrutaban de la misma relación y decidió celebrar la unión familiar con esta historia. Bertrand también escribió *Family, Familia,* un libro sobre dos primos que se conocen en una reunión familiar, y dos deliciosos libros sobre la comida y la familia: *Sip, Slurp, Soup, Soup / Caldo, caldo, caldo* y *The Empanadas that Abuela Made / Las Empanadas que hacía la abuela.* Bertrand vive en San Antonio, Texas con su maravillosa familia.

An Air Force "brat" born to multicultural parents overseas, **Christina E. Rodriguez** grew up loving to draw and paint. She earned her BFA in Illustration from the Rhode Island School of Design in 2003 and presently works as a freelance illustrator and designer. Christina also illustrated *Mayté and the Bogeyman / Mayté y el Cuco* and *Un día con mis tías / A Day with my Aunts* for Piñata Books. She lives with her husband and their dog in historic Stillwater, Minnesota.

Christina E. Rodriguez nació en el extranjero a padres multiculturales, miembros de las Fuerzas Aéreas. Rodriguez creció disfrutando del dibujo y de la pintura. Recibió su BFA de Rhode Island School of Design en 2003 y ahora trabaja como ilustradora y diseñadora independiente. Rodriguez también ilustró *Mayté and the Bogeyman / Mayté y el Cuco* y *Un día con mis tías / A Day with my Aunts* para Piñata Books. Rodriguez vive con su esposo y su perro en Stillwater, Minnesota.